The Perfect Gift

D1012114

#1 It's a Twin Thing
#2 How to Flunk Your First Date
#3 The Sleepover Secret
#4 One Twin Too Many
#5 To Snoop or Not to Snoop
#6 My Sister the Supermodel
#7 Two's a Crowd
#8 Let's Party
#9 Calling All Boys
#10 Winner Take All
#11 P.S. Wish You Were Here
#12 The Cool Club
#13 War of the Wardrobes
#14 Bye-Bye Boyfriend
#15 It's Snow Problem
#16 Likes Me, Likes Me Not
#17 Shore Thing
#18 Two for the Road
#19 Surprise, Surprise!
#20 Sealed With A Kiss
#21 Now You See Him, Now You Don't
#22 April Fools' Rules!
#23 Island Girls
#24 Surf, Sand, and Secrets
#25 Closer Than Ever

The Perfect Gift

by Megan Stine

from the series created by
Robert Griffard
& Howard Adler

HarperEntertainment
An Imprint of **HarperCollins***Publishers*

A PARACHUTE PRESS BOOK

A PARACHUTE PRESS BOOK

Parachute Publishing, L.L.C.
156 Fifth Avenue
Suite 302
New York, NY 10010

Published by
HarperEntertainment
An Imprint of HarperCollins*Publishers*
10 East 53rd Street, New York, NY 10022-5299

TWO OF A KIND books created and produced by Parachute Press, L.L.C., in cooperation with Dualstar Publications, a division of Dualstar Entertainment Group, LLC, published by HarperEntertainment, an imprint of HarperCollins Publishers.

ISBN 0-06-009322-6

HarperCollins®, ® , and HarperEntertainment™ are trademarks of HarperCollins Publishers Inc.

First printing: December 2002

Printed in the United States of America

Visit HarperEntertainment on the World Wide Web at
www.harpercollins.com

10 9 8 7 6 5 4 3 2 1

CHAPTER ONE

"Cheer up!" twelve-year-old Mary-Kate Burke told her friend, Summer Sorenson, as she sat next to her on the bus. "Christmas break is only two weeks away!"

"Easy for you to say," Summer replied glumly. "You didn't flunk Meany Meenan's test on Friday."

"At least I hope I didn't," Mary-Kate said. "That test was tough."

"I'll bet I totally flunked it," Wendy Linden chimed in. "Can you believe he asked that question about the price of lard?"

"That was gross," Elise Van Hook called from the back of the bus.

"I know," Summer said. "I thought that How to

Start Your Own Business was going to be a fun, easy class."

I thought so, too, Mary-Kate silently agreed. *Why couldn't I get an easy class like Ashley?* Her sister was having tons of fun in her Sew What? elective.

Mary-Kate looked out the window and watched the snowy scenery pass by. She and her friends were riding the shuttle bus. It took them from the campus of White Oak Academy—their New Hampshire boarding school for girls—to the Harrington School for Boys next door.

Each year both schools offered special three-week classes right before winter break. Most of them were taught at Harrington.

Short-term classes were usually fun. But How to Start Your Own Business had turned out to be really hard and really serious. The test they took last Friday was a huge part of their grade.

"Well, I refuse to be miserable," Mary-Kate said. "Not with Christmas so close." She could hardly wait for all the holiday treats and parties the schools would be having during the next two weeks. "Besides, Meenan can't fail all of us. Not right before winter break. Right?" she added.

Nobody answered.

Okay, so maybe he could, Mary-Kate realized. *But*

he won't do that. He can't. It would just be too mean!

Mary-Kate glanced across the aisle of the bus. Penelope Marley, a new girl from England, was sitting all by herself. She had just come to White Oak a month ago. Like Mary-Kate, Penelope was in the First Form. That's what they called seventh grade at boarding school.

I'll bet she *didn't fail*, Mary-Kate thought. Penelope was super smart. She had already become Meany Meenan's favorite.

The bus pulled up to the ivy-and-snow-covered stone building where their class was held. Some of the Harrington teachers had hung colored Christmas lights around the archway. Just the sight of them cheered up Mary-Kate.

"See? It's Christmas!" she said as she and her friends hurried into class.

Mr. Meenan was already pacing at the board, scowling. "Take your seats," he said in a gruff voice. "Quickly!"

Uh-oh, Mary-Kate thought. *Not good.* She slid into her seat in the third row—right beside a really nice boy named Carter Black. He had silky blond hair, dark eyes, and rosy cheeks. His skin always looked as if he'd just come in from the cold—even on hot days.

Does he have any idea how cute he is? Mary-Kate

3

wondered with a sigh. She kind of had a crush on him.

"All right, class. I have bad news for you," Mr. Meenan said as he started to hand back the tests. "You all failed."

A small gasp rippled through the classroom.

He corrected himself. "All except Penelope." He handed her test back. "Good work, Penelope. You deserved this A."

Everyone mumbled as the tests came back.

"So," Mr. Meenan said. "I can't let you all fail this class. Well, I could, actually—but it's Christmas. So I'm not going to."

"Yes!" one of the guys said under his breath.

"Don't get excited yet," Mr. Meenan said. "Instead of failing everyone, I'm going to give you all a special holiday gift."

Mary-Kate held her breath. A gift? From Meany Meenan? She didn't like the sound of this.

"I'm giving you all a chance to bring up your grade," he went on, "by assigning you an extra-credit project."

Some of the kids moaned.

"The project is due on the last day of class," Mr. Meenan explained. "You'll split up into teams to work on it. Each team's job is to come up with a holiday product of some sort and then design an advertising campaign for it."

"Huh?" Carter asked. "You want us to sell Christmas stuff?"

"No," Mr. Meenan said. "You don't have to really sell anything. You just have to come up with something that you could sell—and then work up a marketing plan for the item. How much does it cost? How much profit can you make? How many do you need to sell? Who are you going to sell it to? What will the ads look like? See?"

"I see we're in deep trouble," someone cracked from the back of the room, and everyone laughed.

"Well, it's not required," Mr. Meenan said sharply. "But if you don't do the extra-credit project, you'll fail the class."

"This is going to ruin all our holiday fun," Summer grumbled softly to Mary-Kate.

"No way," Mary-Kate whispered back. "It's a good thing. I mean, at least we won't fail the class."

"Okay, let's divide into teams and think about our projects," Mr. Meenan said. Then he called out the names for each group.

Mary-Kate was in Group B. It included Summer Sorenson, Justin Martinez, Seth Samuels, and Carter Black.

All right! Mary-Kate thought when she heard Carter's name called.

"Mr. Meenan?" Penelope said, raising her hand. "May I do the extra-credit project, too?"

"Well, you certainly may," Mr. Meenan said, smiling at her. "But you don't need to. You already have an A in this class."

"I know, but I think it will be good fun!" Penelope said in her crisp British accent.

"Wonderful!" Mr. Meenan clapped his hands. "You can be in Group B."

Summer rolled her eyes at Mary-Kate. "Oh, great. Why do we get stuck with Miss Goody-Teacher's-Pet?"

"Hey, don't complain," Mary-Kate whispered. "Having Penelope on our team is perfect. With her help, we'll get an A for sure!"

"You think so?" Summer's eyes lit up.

"Definitely!" Mary-Kate said.

At least she hoped so!

CHAPTER TWO

"We're going to have the best two weeks ever!" Ashley announced to the huge group of students gathered in front of her.

It was Monday after school. Ashley stood on a chair at the back of the Student Union. All the First Form girls from White Oak were sitting on the couches and chairs. So were the guys from Harrington.

Ashley and the other girls on the Holiday Helper Committee had called this meeting to tell everyone about the holiday events.

"We've got a lot of great stuff planned," Ashley went on. "We'll be having hot cocoa study breaks all week. There's caroling on Thursday night. And next Saturday is the sleigh ride!"

7

"All of us in one sleigh?" Dana Woletsky called out. "I don't think so."

Ashley tried to ignore Dana's remark. Dana Woletsky was just about the only girl at White Oak who Ashley didn't like. Mainly because Dana thought she was the queen of the boarding school!

"We've got two sleighs, and you can sign up for one of the time slots," Ashley explained. "Anyway, here's the best part." She lifted up a large top hat. "We're going to have a gift exchange! Write your name on a little slip of paper and put it in here."

Samantha Kramer, another girl on the committee, passed out little pieces of paper to everyone.

"Then we'll all draw names," Ashley went on.

"Cool!" one of the boys called out. "Whoever gets my name—I want all candy!"

"Whoever gets my name—I want all money!" another boy said.

Ashley laughed. Who had said that?

Oh. Of course. It was her cousin Jeremy. He was always goofing off and playing tricks on people. He didn't take *anything* seriously.

"Here are the rules, "Ashley said. "You draw a name and then you're a Secret Santa for that person. Over the next two weeks, you'll leave the person a gift every few days. There's a five-dollar spending

8

limit on each gift. On the last day of school, we'll have a party and everyone will find out who their Secret Santa is. Okay?"

"I thought we were supposed to vote on the gift exchange," Dana said.

Ashley sighed. She could already tell that everyone wanted to do it, but Dana was right. They were supposed to take a vote.

"Okay. How many people want to do Secret Santa?" Ashley asked.

Every single person in the room raised his or her hand—except for two. Dana and Penelope. Penelope was sitting on a window ledge, off to the side.

Weird, Ashley thought. She knew Dana would vote no, but what was Penelope's problem?

"So put your name in this hat if you want to do the Secret Santa," Ashley said. She moved through the Student U, holding out the hat so everyone could drop their paper in it.

"Awesome idea, Ashley," Mary-Kate said, dropping her paper in the hat.

"Yeah," Summer agreed, flicking hers in as well.

When Ashley got to Dana's group, Dana dropped her name in, too. "I changed my mind," she said coolly.

Finally Ashley reached the corner where

Penelope was sitting. "Don't you want to be part of the gift exchange?" Ashley encouraged her in a friendly voice.

"I think it's silly," Penelope replied. "Besides, I'm going to be quite busy. I have a very important project to do." She glared at Mary-Kate and Summer, who were nearby, talking to Wendy. "I don't know how the rest of you will have time for this nonsense." She got up and walked out.

What was that all about? Ashley wondered.

Wendy rolled her eyes. "Why did she even come if she's going to be such a scrooge?" she said.

"I don't know," Ashley answered. She hurried back to stand on her chair. She shook the hat to mix up all the papers. "Okay, time to draw!" she called.

All at once, everyone came up to take a name from the hat. Some of the boys were pushing and shoving to get closer. They seemed totally into the gift exchange.

Soon Dana stepped up to draw. She smirked as soon as she looked at the name.

Finally it was Ashley's turn. She stirred the few remaining papers with her hands, closed her eyes, and pulled a name out of the hat.

Cheryl Miller.

That's awesome! Ashley thought. Cheryl was a

friend who lived in the same dorm as Ashley.

A few minutes later, the meeting was over. Ashley grabbed her sister's arm in the crowd. "Are you heading back to Porter House?"

"Later," Mary-Kate said. Then she leaned close to Ashley. "I picked Ross's name," she whispered.

"That's cool," Ashley said, although she wished she'd gotten Ross for herself. Ross was Ashley's boyfriend.

Ashley threw on her coat, hat, and mittens. Then she headed out across the beautiful snow-covered campus, to her dorm.

Her room, at the top of the stairs, was warm and bright. And the place was empty. Her roommate, Phoebe Cahill, hadn't come back from the meeting yet. In fact, the whole dorm was quiet.

Perfect! Ashley thought. *I can make a cute card for Cheryl and no one will know.*

She put on some music—a holiday CD. Then she ran down to the drink machine in the dorm lounge to get a grape soda.

"'Sleigh bells ring, are you listenin'," Ashley sang as she ran back upstairs. She opened her desk drawer to get out paper, markers, and glitter. Lying there on top of everything were Cheryl's history notes.

11

"Oops!" Ashley said. She had borrowed the notes last week to study for a test. She had to give them back soon!

Ashley set the notes out on the desk so she wouldn't forget to return them. Then she folded a piece of red paper in half to make a card.

Hmmm . . . what should I write? Ashley glanced at her bottle of glitter. Cheryl used to be in a club called the Glitter Girls. Maybe she could write the whole thing in glitter.

"Dear Cheryl," she began to write. "You are the glitteriest girl in Porter House."

No. Too corny, Ashley decided. Whatever she wrote had to be cool. And she wanted Cheryl to be totally surprised when she opened it.

"Hey. What's up?" a voice said from the doorway. "What are you writing?"

Ashley jerked around. With the music on, she hadn't heard anyone come in. But right in back of her were Phoebe, Mary-Kate, and Cheryl!

CHAPTER THREE

"Oh, hi, there!" Ashley spun back to hide the card on her desk. But in her rush, she knocked over the can of soda—and spilled it all over Cheryl's history notes!

"Oh, no!" Ashley scrambled to grab some tissues to blot up the mess.

"Are those my notes?" Cheryl cried.

"Yes, I'm so sorry!" Ashley apologized. "I was going to bring them back to you today!"

Cheryl grabbed the notes, which were dripping with grape soda. "Now they're all messed up. How am I supposed to study with these?"

Ashley couldn't think of an answer. For a minute, there was an awkward silence.

"I'm really sorry, Cheryl," Ashley apologized again.

Cheryl sighed. "Forget it, Ashley. I know you didn't do it on purpose. See you later." She turned and left the room.

"Hey, Ashley, you won't believe what happened in Meany Meenan's class," Mary-Kate said as they cleaned the grape mess. "He flunked everyone on the test. Well, except Penelope."

"Wow," Phoebe said. "Meenan's giving you tests? I'm taking History in Film. We're just watching old black-and-white movies!"

"So are you going to fail the course?" Ashley asked Mary-Kate.

"No." Mary-Kate quickly told them about the make-up project and the teams. And how Carter was in her group. And how Penelope had volunteered to do the project with them. "I thought it would be great at first, but Penelope wants to have a million meetings to work on it," Mary-Kate explained. "She sent me three e-mails about it already—and we just got the project today!"

"Hey, don't worry about it, Mary-Kate," Ashley replied. "I have three words of advice that will definitely help."

"What?" Mary-Kate asked. "What should I do?"

Ashley picked up her spilled can and smiled. "Avoid . . . grape . . . soda!"

"Mary-Kate, are you even listening?" Penelope asked with her arms folded.

They were sitting in the back of Mr. Meenan's class. All the teams were meeting to discuss their projects. Mary-Kate, Penelope, Summer, Carter, Seth, and Justin were all huddled around a table.

Mary-Kate tucked a strand of blond hair behind her ear and held her head up high. Who did Penelope think she was, talking to her that way? Mary-Kate was beginning to regret voting Penelope as team leader today.

Still, Mary-Kate could feel her face getting red. Penelope was right—she hadn't been listening. She'd been thinking about Carter. About how he had picked a seat right beside her—on purpose. And how cute he looked in his blue-and-black sweater.

Mary-Kate cleared her throat. "Of course I am," she replied.

"We have to come up with a product to sell," Penelope said. "Does anyone have any other ideas?"

"How about paper snowflakes?" Summer suggested. "You know, to hang in your window as a holiday decoration."

"Dumb," Justin said. "I wouldn't buy one. Would you?"

"No," Mary-Kate agreed. "I wouldn't buy something I could make myself."

"You can make paper snowflakes?" Summer said, sounding impressed.

"Even I can make a paper snowflake." Carter laughed.

"How about holiday cookies?" Mary-Kate suggested.

"No way," Summer teased her. "Not with your baking skills."

"That's true," Mary-Kate replied, and smiled. She was a disaster in the kitchen. "But we don't have to really make the cookies. Mr. Meenan said we just need an idea."

"I say no to the cookies as well. We have to come up with something better than that," Penelope argued. "Something no one else has. And I have an idea."

"Spit it out," Justin demanded.

Penelope got a pleased-with-herself smile on her face. "Well," she said, "you all seem to like those frightful holiday songs. So what if we sold something that plays the silly tunes every time a person opens their door?"

"You mean like those greeting cards that play music when you open them?" Seth asked.

"Exactly," Penelope said.

"Cool, but how are we going to do that?" Justin asked. "I mean, it takes some kind of computer technology, doesn't it?"

Penelope nodded. "It's a tiny computer chip," she explained. "My mother runs a company that sells novelties. Right now she's in Hong Kong. I'll ask her to send us a sample overnight."

"Seriously?" Mary-Kate said. "That's awesome!" She was beginning to get excited about the project.

Mr. Meenan was walking around the classroom, listening to each group's ideas. Just then he came over to their table. "How are you doing?" he asked.

"Great," Mary-Kate said. "Penelope came up with a fabulous idea." She described the plan.

"I like it!" Mr. Meenan said. "Yes, this is good. In fact. . ." He marched to front of the room.

"Class, I have an announcement to make," he said. "I'm hearing so many good ideas from you all that I think we need to do something special. On the last day before winter break, we're going to hold an assembly. You'll all get to present your extra-credit projects in front of the First Form students and teachers of both schools."

That'll be fun, Mary-Kate thought.

Penelope pulled out her weekly planner. "Well, now the pressure is really on," she said. "We've got to be perfect! So we're going to need lots of meetings. How about tomorrow after school?"

"I can't tomorrow," Justin said. "I've got a paper to write for English."

"Well, how about right after our last class today?" Penelope asked.

"I've got chorus practice at three-thirty," Summer said. "And then Phipps House is baking holiday cookies, and they invited Porter House to come munch."

Penelope sighed. "How about tonight?"

"That sounds good to me," Mary-Kate said quickly. "As long as we can make the holiday hot cocoa break in the Student U. We don't want to miss that!"

Penelope dropped her pencil and scowled. "If we want to be good, we have to work. We don't have time for hot cocoa."

"But—" Mary-Kate began.

"Do you want me to be the team leader or not?" Penelope interrupted.

Everyone nodded.

"Well, then we'll get together tonight," she said firmly. "And we'll meet again on Thursday, while everyone's out caroling."

"Can't we meet sometime when there isn't a fun holiday activity going on?" Summer said.

"No," Penelope said. "Like my mother always says: Work first, play later."

Everyone just stared at her.

What is her problem? Mary-Kate wondered. It's almost as if Penelope wanted to ruin their holiday fun. Then she thought of something else. Maybe she was just lonely. Maybe she just needed some time to get used to White Oak.

"I don't mind missing one or two holiday things," Carter spoke up. "But everything? No way, Penelope."

"Well, if it's more important to go caroling, then go ahead," Penelope replied. "But I'm dropping out. You all can do the project on your own."

Mary-Kate's eyes opened wide. Dropping out? But how could they do the cool musical door opener without her? They needed her mom for that.

And now that they'd told Mr. Meenan about their project, he was counting on them.

"Okay." Mary-Kate gave in. "We can meet somewhere tonight." She looked at Carter. "Right?"

"Yeah," Carter said glumly. "Okay."

"Whatever," Justin said. "But the Student U will be packed. So where are we going to meet?"

"We can use the library," Penelope said.

"Oh, great," Summer said. "Just where I wanted

to spend the best moments of the holiday season."

The bell rang, and Penelope got up to leave. As soon as she was gone, everyone in the group started grumbling. Everyone except Seth. He was pretty quiet.

"I thought it was going to be easier with her on our team," Justin said. "But she's making it harder!"

"True. But what can we do?" Summer said. "I need a good grade in this class."

"But we're going to miss out on all the fun," Carter said, looking right at Mary-Kate.

Wow, Mary-Kate thought. *Did that mean what I think it meant? That he wants to be having fun hanging out with* me? Her heart skipped a beat.

"Don't worry," she said. "I'll try to talk to Penelope and get her to lighten up. We won't miss out on everything."

"Could you?" Summer said. "That would be great. But good luck. She's a grinch."

Mary-Kate shook her head. "She's probably just feeling a little homesick—or left out—because she's new at school. All I have to do is make her feel welcome here," she added. "I can get her into the holiday spirit for sure."

CHAPTER FOUR

"Aren't you going to open it?" Ashley asked Phoebe. She pointed to the small wrapped box in Phoebe's hand. The two of them were walking toward the dining hall for lunch.

"I'm waiting for you to get yours," Phoebe said, "So we can open them together." She held up the gift. "I found this sitting on my chair when I got to math class."

Ashley shivered. A bitter wind blew a light dusting of snow in her face. "Secret Santa is so much fun!" she said. "I can't wait to get my first present."

Ashley and Phoebe reached the dining hall. Inside, the whole place was buzzing. Everyone seemed to be in a great mood, thanks to their Secret

Santas. Ashley saw torn wrapping paper and ribbons everywhere.

"Look what I got!" Mary-Kate rushed up to Ashley. "Baseball cards!"

"That's so perfect!" Ashley said. Mary-Kate was a great athlete. Her favorite sport was baseball.

"Your Secret Santa must have known that you'd really like those," Ashley said. "Do you have any idea who it is?"

Mary-Kate shook her head. "I don't even want to guess yet."

"Guessing is the fun part," Ashley said as she and Phoebe found a table and put their things down.

"I know, but it's not fun if you figure it out too soon," Mary-Kate said. "Anyway, I'll catch you later!"

"Okay." Ashley nodded and took off her coat, hat, and mittens.

Now I have hat hair, she realized. She could feel it. Her hair was plastered against her head. She reached into her backpack for a comb. At the bottom, she felt something strange.

"Hey—look!" she cried.

Hidden in the bottom of her backpack was a beautiful little present wrapped up with silver foil and gold ribbon.

The Perfect Gift

"Your Secret Santa?" Phoebe said.

Ashley nodded, smiling. "I wonder who it is. . . ."

She tried to think. Who could have put a gift in there? And when? She'd had her backpack with her all morning.

"Let's open our presents," Phoebe suggested. "On the count of three. One . . . two . . ."

"Three!" Ashley cried, and tore off the wrapping paper.

Phoebe opened her box first. "Cookies!" she announced. "Home-baked chocolate chip."

"Yum." Ashley could smell them. And they smelled good!

"I'll share," Phoebe promised.

"Now me!" Ashley said, excited. Her face beamed as she opened the lid to her box. But when she saw the gift, she frowned.

Inside was an ugly old crumpled paper napkin on top of something lumpy.

"What is that?" Phoebe asked.

"I don't know," Ashley said. She lifted up the napkin.

Underneath was a disgusting, half-eaten bologna sandwich.

"Gross!" Phoebe said.

"I know," Ashley said. She tried to stay positive.

"Maybe it was just an accident. Maybe my Secret Santa was in a big hurry and put the wrong sandwich in there by mistake or something."

"Hmmm," Phoebe said. She didn't sound sure.

Or maybe my Secret Santa just didn't plan ahead, Ashley thought. *Maybe she didn't have time to get me a gift, so she gave me a leftover sandwich.*

There was probably a good reason for this.

At least Ashley hoped so!

She picked up the sandwich and the wrapping paper and walked over to the trash to throw it away. Just then, Dana passed by. When she caught sight of the gross sandwich, she snickered. "Don't like your gift?" she asked with a laugh.

Ashley narrowed her eyes. Was Dana her Secret Santa? She hoped not. That would be a total bummer!

For the rest of the day, Ashley tried to stay in a good mood. But it was hard. Everyone else seemed to be getting really great gifts.

Elise Van Hook found a collection of little sample-size bottles of bath stuff tucked in her coat pocket. Samantha got a solid piece of chocolate in the shape of her initial. And someone had given Summer a pretty friendship bracelet made with pink string and black beads.

That's okay, Ashley thought. *They all deserve nice gifts. I'll probably get something better tomorrow.*

But the next day, she didn't get anything at all. Not in the morning, anyway.

At lunch, she looked in her backpack twice, but there were no cards or presents hidden there.

"Did you check your mailbox?" Mary-Kate said when classes were over. The two of them were hanging out in Ashley's room. "Maybe your Secret Santa put something in there."

"No," Ashley said. "Do you think I should?"

Mary-Kate nodded. "It's worth a try."

Right, Ashley thought. She ran downstairs to the large wooden case at the back of the dorm lobby.

"You were right!" she called up the stairs.

There, stuffed into the slot with her name, was another wrapped package. Ashley grabbed it and ran back up to her room.

"At least it's too big to be a half-eaten sandwich," Ashley said.

"Unless it's two half-eaten sandwiches," Mary-Kate joked.

Ashley tore off the wrapping. Inside was a pair of stinky, dirty old gym socks!

"Oh, no!" Mary-Kate cried when she saw them.

Ashley threw the socks on the floor. "That's not

fair!" she said. "Secret Santa isn't supposed to be a way to hurt someone's feelings. It's supposed to be a way to show holiday spirit!"

"I know," Mary-Kate said. "Whoever did this is totally mean."

Ashley flopped down on her bed and sighed. *Who would do this to me?* she wondered. Who would give her two really nasty presents? They had to be from someone who didn't like her. But who didn't like her?

Then Ashley remembered Dana. It was no secret that she and Ashley weren't exactly friends.

Please, please, please don't let Dana be my Secret Santa!

CHAPTER FIVE

"Did you figure it out yet?" Mary-Kate asked Ashley the next morning at breakfast.

The two of them were sitting in the dining hall, eating the standard White Oak breakfast—oatmeal. They ate oatmeal almost every single day of the school year.

"No," Ashley said. "I mean, maybe. There's only one person I don't get along with."

Mary-Kate nodded. "That's what I was thinking, too."

"And there she is now," Ashley said. Dana and her best friend, Kristen Lindquist, were walking into the dining hall. They both had snow all over their coats.

Dana walked by and gave them a dirty look.

Mary-Kate leaned forward. "Do you really think she'd have the nerve to give you such horrible presents?" she asked. "I mean, that's pretty bad, even for her!"

"I don't know," Ashley said. "I can't think of anyone else. Can you?"

Mary-Kate shook her head. Everyone liked Ashley. There wasn't another person at White Oak or Harrington who didn't. "So what are you going to do?" Mary-Kate asked.

Ashley shrugged. "I don't know. I guess I'll have to catch her delivering a gift or something. Then I'll know for sure if she's my Secret Santa."

Right, Mary-Kate thought. That was the only way.

"So ask me how my business project is going," Mary-Kate said.

"Okay. How's your business project going?" Ashley asked.

"Wonderful! I mean, the meetings are great, anyway," Mary-Kate gushed.

"Wow!" Ashley said. "That's great. I guess you started liking Penelope's meetings better?"

"Not really," Mary-Kate admitted. "But Carter has been sitting next to me in every single meeting.

And yesterday he asked me to study with him for finals!"

"Cool," Ashley said. "So you like him?"

"What do you think?" Mary-Kate asked. A smile spread across her face. Carter wasn't just cute. He was funny, too. And nice.

"So maybe he'll go with you on one of the sleigh rides," Ashley said. "You should sign up for a nighttime ride. Which reminds me—I need to make the sign-up sheets."

"I'll help you with that tonight," Mary-Kate said. "But I might not be able to even go on a sleigh ride. Not if Penelope has her way."

"You have to go!" Ashley said. "The sleigh rides are going to be awesome!"

"I know," Mary-Kate agreed. "But Penelope says we have to work on our project every waking minute."

"Can't you talk to her?" Ashley asked.

"I'm supposed to," Mary-Kate said with a nod. "I mean, I promised everyone in the group that I'd get her to lighten up."

"Well, now's your chance," Ashley said. She nodded toward a table at the far end of the dining hall. "There she is."

Mary-Kate turned to look. Penelope was sitting alone. *Okay*. Mary-Kate stood up. *It's now or never*.

"Wish me luck!" She walked across the dining hall to Penelope's table and sat down.

"Hey," Mary-Kate said.

"Hi." Penelope smiled.

Mary-Kate glanced at the stack of books Penelope had sitting beside her. There were seven or eight at least.

"My gosh, you have so much work!" Mary-Kate said, staring at the books.

"Oh, that's not all work," Penelope said. "I'm reading three of those for fun."

"Speaking of fun," Mary-Kate said, "I wanted to talk to you."

"About what?" Penelope asked.

"I was thinking," Mary-Kate said. "You should come caroling with the chorus tonight. Everyone's allowed to join in and—"

"No thanks." Penelope cut her off. "All that stuff is silly."

"Oh, but it's not!" Mary-Kate insisted. "It's really fun! I mean, the holidays are all about being together, and sharing and everything! Why don't you—"

"Why don't you mind your own business!" Penelope snapped. "You have no right to tell me how to celebrate the holidays!"

Whoa, Mary-Kate thought. *Why did she get so*

angry all of a sudden? Maybe she's just afraid to join in.

"Look, why don't you try it before you say it's not fun," Mary-Kate urged her. "At least come to the Student U tonight. There's a hot cocoa break after the caroling. And we're having a contest to guess how many chocolate coins are in a jar. Whoever guesses the closest gets all the candy."

"That's so babyish," Penelope snapped; "and very stupid."

I don't believe her! Mary-Kate thought. *That contest was my idea. Is she calling me a stupid baby?*

"Next you'll be telling me you're playing peek-a-boo with an elf," Penelope went on. "How childish are you?"

"Hey," Mary-Kate said. "Just because you're a grump and a scrooge about the holidays doesn't mean you have to make fun of everyone else!"

"Did you just call me a scrooge?" Penelope asked coldly.

"Yes!" Mary-Kate replied.

"Fine." Penelope stared at Mary-Kate. "If you think I'm such a scrooge, then maybe you should do the business project yourself! I quit!"

Uh-oh, Mary-Kate thought. *That didn't turn out the way I'd hoped. Not at all!*

• • •

"Ashley! Look what I found on your bed!" Phoebe announced, marching into the Porter House lounge.

Ashley looked up from her magazine. She was curled in a chair, checking out the latest issue of *Cool It* magazine.

"Your Secret Santa strikes again!" Phoebe held out a small box wrapped in red, green, and gold paper.

"Does it smell funny?" Ashley asked, eyeing the package carefully.

Phoebe took a whiff. "Nope. Smells safe."

"Okay. Give it to me." Ashley took the box reluctantly.

She glanced around the lounge to see who was watching. A few girls were huddled in one corner, eating popcorn. Another group from Phipps House was hanging around near the door.

Ashley spotted Kristen, Dana's best friend.

Was Dana there, too? Was she just waiting and watching to laugh at Ashley's gift?

Ashley didn't want to open it in front of everyone. But she didn't want to be a chicken about it, either.

"Come on," Phoebe said, encouraging her. "I bet it's something really nice this time."

I hope so, Ashley thought. She tore off the wrapping and held up the gift. It was a pair of really ugly pointed elf ears. Big rubber things that you could wear for a costume—if you were a total geek. Or out of your mind.

"Great." Ashley frowned. She tossed them to Phoebe.

"Oh," Phoebe said as if she couldn't think of anything else to say.

Then Ashley heard the girls in the hall laughing. And Dana's voice came through loud and strong.

"Aren't Ashley's presents the worst?" Dana said. "I think they're hilarious!"

The other girls in the hall laughed and ran upstairs.

"What's she doing here?" Phoebe asked.

"I don't know," Ashley said, "but I have my suspicions. I saw her lurking around outside our room a few hours ago."

Phoebe nodded. "Now that you mention it, I saw her near our room yesterday. And she was downstairs near the mailboxes, too!"

"So that settles it," Ashley said, gritting her teeth.

"What?" Phoebe's eyes opened wide. "You think Dana's your Secret Santa?"

"I'm sure of it!" Ashley announced. "And I'm going to get her back if it's the last thing I do!"

CHAPTER SIX

Ashley had to hurry if she was going to catch the bus to Harrington.

But first she had a Secret Santa gift to deliver.

She peeked out into the hall to make sure all the other girls had left the dorm. Then she hurried up to the third floor, where Cheryl's room was.

She's really going to like this, Ashley thought as she left the gift outside Cheryl's door.

It was a little pouch filled with lavender potpourri. Ashley had attached a card telling Cheryl to put the pouch in her drawers. It would make them smell nice.

"Ashley? Are you still up there?" Phoebe called from downstairs. "You're going to miss the bus!"

Ashley ran downstairs, and the two of them dashed out the front door.

"Phew," Ashley said, jumping onto the bus with Phoebe just in time.

"Did you get a gift this morning?" Phoebe asked.

Ashley shook her head no. "You?"

Phoebe opened her notebook and pulled out a piece of paper. "I got this photocopy of a magazine cover from the 1940s to put on my wall. Isn't it cool?"

Ashley nodded. *It's way more than cool*, she thought. Phoebe was totally into vintage stuff. Her gift was really considerate. And thoughtful.

The complete opposite of the gifts Ashley had gotten!

When the bus stopped, the girls hurried into the building. A bunch of Harrington boys were hanging around in the hall outside class.

"Hi," Ross said, smiling at Ashley. "Are we going on the sleigh ride tomorrow night?"

"Definitely!" Ashley said. "I signed us up for seven o'clock. Is that okay?"

"Sure," Ross said. He pulled a CD out of his messenger bag. "Maybe I'll bring this and we can listen to it in the Student U after the sleigh ride."

"What is it?" Ashley asked. But she already knew.

"It's from my Secret Santa. It has all my favorite

songs on it," he said. "I mean, every single song I love."

He shot her a questioning look that said, *Did you give this to me?*

Ashley smiled. She had told Mary-Kate what songs to put on the CD.

"Great," Ashley said. "I can't wait to hear it."

Ross grinned, trying to figure out if she was faking or not.

"'Here comes Santa Claus, here comes Santa Claus,'" someone sang behind Ashley.

She turned around and saw her cousin Jeremy walking toward her. He was holding something behind his back.

"Ho, ho, ho!" Jeremy said in a big, phony Santa voice. "Here's a present for little Ashley Burke from your secret Holiday Helper."

"Huh?" Ashley looked at him.

Jeremy smiled. "Your Secret Santa asked me to give you . . . this!" He pulled his hand out from behind his back and handed her a lump of coal.

"Coal? Are you kidding?" Ashley said. This was the last straw! "Who told you to give that to me?" she demanded.

"I'll never tell," Jeremy said, his eyes twinkling.

"Come on, Jeremy," Ashley insisted. "Tell me! It was Dana, wasn't it?"

Jeremy laughed and pretended to button up his lips. "I'm sworn to secrecy," he said.

"Jeremy, I mean it. Tell me who gave you that piece of coal!"

"Why, Ashley," he said, pretending to be shocked. "I can't believe you would want to spoil your Secret Santa surprise!"

Jeremy was being impossible. But Ashley knew from the sly grin on his face that she had guessed correctly.

It was Dana, all right. No one else would dare do something this mean during the holidays!

"Okay," Ashley said under her breath to Phoebe. "I know what to do get her back. Are you in?"

"What's going on?" Ross asked.

"Nothing," Ashley said. "Just something I've got to handle myself. With Phoebe's help."

"I'm in," Phoebe answered softly. Then the bell rang.

All through biology, Ashley thought about her revenge. After class, she and Phoebe rode back on the bus together. They sat alone in the back corner so no one could hear them.

"So what's your plan?" Phoebe asked.

"Simple," Ashley said. "You know how Dana has a pizza party in her room every Friday night?"

Phoebe nodded.

"Why don't we change her order and send her a really gross pizza instead?" Ashley suggested.

"Great idea," Phoebe said.

"But can you help me?" Ashley asked. "You hang out in Phipps House tomorrow night and find out when they order the pizza. Then I'll call and change the order."

"Okay," Phoebe agreed. "They always order pepperoni, veggie, and extra cheese."

Ashley nodded. "I know. But as soon as they put in the order, I'll change it to anchovies, onions, and jalapeño peppers!"

Phoebe grinned and gave Ashley a low-five so no one on the bus would see.

Serves Dana right, Ashley thought. *She's going to get a Christmas surprise that will teach her a lesson for sure!*

CHAPTER SEVEN

"What do you mean, she isn't coming?" Carter asked. He checked his watch for the third time in two minutes.

It was Friday, just one week before the extra-credit project was due. Mr. Meenan was letting each group meet during class. But Penelope was nowhere in sight.

Mary-Kate shifted in her seat. "Penelope decided to drop out," she explained. "Mr. Meenan let her go to the library since she's not working on the project."

"But why did she quit?" Justin asked.

I've got to tell them, Mary-Kate thought. But how could she explain that it was all her fault Penelope

39

quit? And now they were stuck without the smartest person on the team?

Just tell the truth, Mary-Kate decided. That was always the best way.

"It's my fault," Mary-Kate admitted. "Remember when I said I'd talk to her? And get her to lighten up on all the meetings?"

Carter nodded. "What happened?"

"Well, basically she called me stupid and I called her a scrooge and then she quit," Mary-Kate blurted out.

"Hey, I say good-bye and good riddance," Justin said.

"Ditto," Summer chimed in.

"I didn't like her anyway," Seth said, speaking up for the first time.

Mary-Kate glanced at Carter.

"No problem," he said. "We don't need her. She already gave us that musical thing her mom sent from Hong Kong."

"Really?" Mary-Kate asked. "So you guys aren't mad at me?"

Carter put his arm around her. "I say you'll make a better team leader any day."

Seriously? Mary-Kate couldn't believe he was being so nice!

"So let's get busy," Justin said. "Where is that musical thing anyway?"

Carter reached for his backpack. The minute he touched it, the music started to play.

"It's in here," he said. "She gave it to me at the last meeting. But it's really touchy. If you even bump it . . ."

The thing was playing "Jingle Bells" really fast, over and over.

". . . it starts, and won't stop," Carter explained.

"Can't you turn it off?" Summer asked.

Carter shook her head. "It's triggered by motion. Any little motion. I mean, sometimes it plays when you don't even go near it."

"Great," Summer said. "Maybe we should put that in our ad campaign. It could say something like 'Did you ever wish Christmas would never end? Well, now it won't!'"

Carter laughed. "Or how about 'Jingle all the way . . . to the end of time!'"

"Okay," Mary-Kate said when the music finally stopped. "Now let's get serious. Come on—we've got to come up with a good ad campaign."

"How about 'Buy our musical door opener'?" Summer suggested.

"Uh . . . no," Carter said. He accidentally touched

his bag with his foot and the music started all over again.

Everyone groaned.

For the next forty minutes, they tried to brainstorm. But none of their ideas were very good. By the time the bell rang, everyone was pretty upset.

"Why don't we just use my idea?" Summer said. "'Buy our musical door opener.'"

"Our project is going to bomb," Justin said matter-of-factly.

"No, it's not," Mary-Kate argued. "Don't worry, we'll think of something. We just have to keep working at it. Maybe we should meet again after school," she suggested.

But when they did, they still came up with nothing. And Mary-Kate was getting a headache from the door opener. Justin had picked it up and had set off the music—six times!

"We're going to look like idiots on Friday," Carter said. "We can't get up in front of the whole school with a boring ad campaign."

"I think we should ask Penelope to come back," Seth said.

Mary-Kate stared at him. "I thought you said you didn't like her."

Seth shrugged. "I don't, but she's got good ideas. I think we need her."

"Maybe Seth is right," Carter agreed. "After all, the musical-door-opener thing was Penelope's idea. She can probably help us come up with ideas for a great ad."

Mary-Kate thought about it. She didn't have a good idea. Nobody did. And she had a feeling that nobody would.

The group was in trouble. They needed Penelope.

"So, how are you going to ask Penelope to come back?" Justin asked Mary-Kate.

"Me?" Mary-Kate replied. "Why do I have to do it?"

"Well, it is kind of your fault that she left in the first place," Justin said. "And you are the team leader. . . ."

"All right, all right," Mary-Kate agreed. "I'll ask her."

"Good," Seth said right away.

"And you can take this thing with you," Carter said, handing her the musical chip.

The minute he lifted it, it started playing again.

Mary-Kate sighed. *Campbell's going to love me when I bring that into our room!* she thought. *And*

43

how am I going to get Penelope to rejoin the group?

That was the big question.

And she didn't have an answer—yet.

"Wow!" Ashley said. She stared at the sparkly bracelet on Mary-Kate's arm. "That's so pretty! When did you get it?"

"I found it wrapped up in my coat pocket after my business class today," Mary-Kate explained.

"So do you think your Secret Santa is in your class?" Ashley asked.

"Maybe," Mary-Kate said. "But I told you—I don't want to know. I'm having too much fun getting these presents."

"But aren't you even curious?" Ashley asked.

"Sort of," Mary-Kate admitted. "But I've got other stuff on my mind." She told Ashley about the latest Penelope problem.

"Hmmm." Ashley said, but she was only half listening. She glanced at the clock on her dresser. It was almost eight o'clock on Friday night.

She and Phoebe had come back from Phipps about twenty minutes ago. Then Ashley had called in the yucky pizza order.

It should be arriving at Dana's room any minute, Ashley thought. She giggled, thinking about it. She

44

could hardly wait to hear how Dana's pizza party had been ruined!

"What are you laughing about?" Mary-Kate asked.

Ashley paused. Then she got up and closed the door. She wanted to tell Mary-Kate, but she didn't want anyone on the floor to hear.

"You know how we thought Dana was the one sending me those horrible gifts?" Ashley whispered. "Well, I figured out how to get her back. Phoebe and I switched her pizza order for tonight. She's going to get anchovies, onions, and jalapeño peppers!"

"No, she's not," Mary-Kate said.

"Yes, she is," Ashley said. "I changed the pizza order myself."

"No. Dana's not your Secret Santa," Mary-Kate said. "I'm positive. I saw her putting a gift next door, in Megan's room."

"What?" Ashley froze. "Are you serious?"

Mary-Kate nodded. "I'm sorry I forgot to tell you!"

"Oh, no!" Ashley felt her throat tighten up. She'd made a terrible mistake. She'd totally blamed Dana for something she didn't do!

No wonder Dana was hanging around Porter House

so much, Ashley thought. She was delivering gifts—to someone else!

And now a yucky pizza was going to arrive at her room any minute!

"Got to go, Mary-Kate!" Ashley leaped up and grabbed her coat. Then she ran to the lounge to find Phoebe.

"Phoebe! I've made a terrible mistake!" Ashley whispered in her ear. "Dana's not my Secret Santa!"

"She's not?" Phoebe's eyes opened wide.

"No!" Ashley said. "Come on! We've got to stop that pizza before it's too late!"

CHAPTER EIGHT

Phoebe didn't even grab her coat. She just jammed on her shoes and followed Ashley to the door.

"What if we're too late?" Ashley said, dashing out into the cold, dark night.

"We're not!" Phoebe cried. "There's the pizza guy now!"

In the moonlight, Ashley saw the red, white, and blue hat on the pizza delivery guy. He was just opening the door of Phipps House, the dorm next to Porter.

"Let's go!" Ashley cried, running.

She and Phoebe ran as fast as they could across the icy, slippery walk. When they reached Phipps, they dashed inside.

"Hey! Wait!" they called to the guy, who was already up one flight of stairs.

The pizza guy didn't stop. Music blared from one of the girl's rooms. The music drowned out the sound of her voice.

Dana's room was on the top floor. Ashley took the steps two at a time.

"Hey!" she called again, running up to the guy just as he was about to knock on Dana's door.

"What?" the guy said, staring at her.

"Uh, that's my pizza," Ashley said.

He looked her up and down, staring at her coat. "You're Dana Woletsky? Is this is your room?" he asked, nodding toward the door. He looked as if he doubted it.

"Uh, no, but I ordered that, and—anyway, it's a long story," Ashley said. She pulled some money out of her coat pocket and shoved it into his hands. "Here. Let me pay for that."

"Okay," the guy said, giving her the yucky pizza.

"And can you go back to Pizza Palace and get a large pizza with pepperoni, veggies, and extra cheese? And bring it back here fast—to Dana's room?" Ashley begged.

"Whatever," the guy said with a shrug.

Ashley let out a sigh of relief. "Thanks. Thanks a

lot. And don't, um, don't tell anyone about this, okay?"

The guy shrugged again, then started down the stairs.

"Let's get out of here before someone sees us!" Phoebe whispered to Ashley.

Ashley nodded, and the two of them hurried out of the dorm.

As soon as they were outside, Ashley moaned. "I am so bummed!" she cried. "I just wasted twelve dollars on this gross pizza. And I still don't know who my Secret Santa is!"

"Yeah," Phoebe agreed.

"I mean, I thought Dana was the only one who hated me," Ashley went on. "I try so hard to be nice to everyone."

"You are! You're nicer than I am," Phoebe agreed. "Is anyone mad at you?"

Ashley thought about that. "No," she said. "Why would anyone be mad at me?"

Phoebe shrugged. "I don't know. Did you steal anyone's boyfriend or borrow someone's sweater and forget to give it back?"

"No." Ashley shook her head.

"How about gossiping?" Phoebe asked. "Did you spread any terrible rumors?"

"Not this month!" Ashley joked.

"Hmmm," Phoebe said. "Just as I thought. You're perfect."

"No, I'm not," Ashley said.

"Well, what have you done to anyone to make them mad?" Phoebe asked.

"Nothing," Ashley started to say. But then she remembered Cheryl.

Cheryl had been really annoyed when Ashley spilled grape soda all over her history notes.

"Wait, maybe it's Cheryl," Ashley said slowly. "And now that I think about it, Cheryl hasn't really been around Porter House all week. She usually stops by my room at least once a day." She gasped. "What if she never forgave me for spilling soda on her history notes?"

"Ohhh," Phoebe said as she pulled open the front door of Porter House. "Do you think she's your Secret Santa?"

"I don't know," Ashley said, stomping the snow off her feet inside the dorm. "Maybe she *is* my Secret Santa. She's the only person I can think of who's mad at me."

Ashley felt terrible. She was so sorry she had ruined Cheryl's notes.

"Oh, gosh," Phoebe said. "What are you going to

do? I mean, you don't want to get back at her, do you?"

"No!" Ashley said quickly. "No way. I want to make it up to her. Somehow I've got to find a way to show Cheryl that I'm really sorry—so she won't hate me!"

CHAPTER NINE

"You're so wet!" Mary-Kate's mouth fell open when she saw her sister coming in from outside on Sunday afternoon.

"I know. I'm soaked!" Ashley laughed. "The snow went right through my jeans! And my hair is dripping. And my hands are freezing!"

Then why does she look so happy? Mary-Kate wondered as she followed her sister into her room. "Where have you been?"

"Sledding down Mulberry Hill on cafeteria trays," Ashley said. "Did you forget? It was on the schedule of holiday activities for one o'clock today."

Mary-Kate sighed. Her shoulders slumped. "I didn't exactly forget," she said. "I didn't have time to even think about it. My business group had to meet after lunch today."

"Not again!" Ashley looked amazed. "But you're missing everything!"

"Don't rub it in," Mary-Kate begged.

Ashley pulled off her wet jeans and changed into some dry clothes. "So how's it going, anyway?" she asked.

"Terribly," Mary-Kate admitted. "We haven't come up with a way to present the whole thing—and really sell it. We're going to fail this class if we don't come up with something good soon."

"Oh, no," Ashley asked. "Do you have any ideas?"

"Well, everyone thinks we should ask Penelope to come back to the group," Mary-Kate said. "I'm supposed to talk to her, but I haven't been able to find her."

"She hangs out in her room a lot," Ashley said. "Did you try there?"

Mary-Kate nodded. "I looked for her this morning after oatmeal, but she was gone."

Mary-Kate gazed around Ashley's room while Ashley toweled her hair. She spotted something glittery and decorated on Ashley's desk.

"What's this?" Mary-Kate asked. "Did your

Secret Santa send you a nice card or something?"

"Oh, no," Ashley said. "Those are Cheryl's history notes. I sneaked into Cheryl's room this morning and borrowed them again. I'm copying them over for her—with colored markers, and stickers, and glitter and everything. So they'll look nice. You know, to make it up to her."

"That's cool," Mary-Kate said.

Ashley nodded. "But it's a surprise, so don't tell."

"I won't." Mary-Kate stood up. "Well, I'd better go see if Penelope's in her room."

But Mary-Kate had a feeling that Penelope wouldn't come back to the group. Why should she? She didn't need the extra credit.

"You want me to come with you?" Ashley offered. "For moral support."

"Would you?" Mary-Kate smiled gratefully. "That would be excellent."

Ashley nodded and put a shiny clip in her hair. They headed for the door. "Look on the bright side," she said as they walked down the hall toward the back stairway. "At least you're getting to spend tons of time with Carter."

"True." Mary-Kate grinned. "He's soooo nice. And I'm pretty sure he has a crush on me, too."

"Really?" Ashley said.

"Well, he asked me to hang out with him at the Student U tonight," Mary-Kate said.

"Excellent!" Ashley said. "Maybe I'll see you there. Ross and I are going."

The girls climbed the stairs to the third floor and found Penelope's room. She wasn't there, but her door was open.

Mary-Kate peeked into the room and spotted Penelope's weekly planner lying open on her desk.

She's like a banker or something, Mary-Kate thought. She had seen Penelope writing down every single minute of her daily schedule in that book.

"Maybe I can find out where she is," Mary-Kate said, checking out the planner.

Ashley followed her into the room. She gazed into Penelope's open closet. "Wow. She's got some awesome sweaters in there. Funny, I never realized it—but she wears some really cool things, doesn't she?"

"I never noticed," Mary-Kate mumbled as she read the planner page.

Let's see, Mary-Kate thought. Today was Sunday. According to the schedule, Penelope would be in a meeting of the White Oak Library Volunteers right now.

Oh, well. I can't barge in on her meeting, Mary-Kate

thought. She glanced down the page. Hmmm. Penelope didn't have anything planned for five o'clock.

Maybe she'll come back to her room and I can catch her then, Mary-Kate decided. Then her eyes wandered to a letter lying open on Penelope's desk. Actually, it wasn't a letter. It was a printed-out e-mail. But it was signed, "Love, Mom."

"What are you doing?" Ashley asked, catching Mary-Kate snooping. Ashley raced over to the desk. "Are you reading her private stuff?"

"I can't help it," Mary-Kate said. "Look!" She didn't touch the letter or anything. She just bent her head over the desk.

Ashley did the same thing. The letter said:

Dear Penelope,

I'm so terribly sorry to have to write to you about our Christmas plans. Unfortunately, I have an emergency business trip at the end of December. I'll be going to China for the holidays, so I won't be able to pick you up at White Oak as we had planned. I'm sure you'll understand—you know how business is! But don't worry, dear. You won't be alone. I've arranged for you to spend the holidays with your great-aunt Prudence—just like you always do. You and she will go to her lovely little island off the coast of Maine.

I'm sure you'll have a wonderful time. I'll be missing you and thinking about you. And I'll send a surprise!

Love,
Mom

"How awful!" Mary-Kate gasped. "Her mother won't even come home to see her at Christmas!"

"No wonder Penelope's been such a scrooge!" Ashley agreed. "She must hate the holidays. I'll bet she's totally lonely every year—stuck with her old aunt on some island."

Poor thing, Mary-Kate thought. Now that she knew why Penelope was so grumpy, she felt awful.

Mary-Kate tore a piece of paper out of a note-book on Penelope's desk. She wrote a quick letter.

Dear Penelope,

Please come back to our group and help us with our project. We really miss you and need you! You're the best!

Thanks,
Mary-Kate
P.S. I'm sorry I called you a scrooge.

"There," Mary-Kate said, showing the note to Ashley. "What do you think?"

"I think it will work," Ashley said.

I hope so, Mary-Kate thought. She left the note on the desk. Then she started to tiptoe out of Penelope's room.

But at the door, she turned around. "You know what? I'm going to leave this bracelet for her," Mary-Kate said. She ran back to the desk and slipped the sparkly bracelet off her arm.

"Isn't that the one your Secret Santa gave you?" Ashley said.

"Yes," Mary-Kate said. "And I love it. But I think Penelope needs it more. She doesn't have a Secret Santa."

"Oh, yes, she does," Ashley said.

"She does?" Mary-Kate asked. "Who?"

"You!" Ashley said, giving her sister a proud smile.

I just hope my gift makes Penelope feel wanted, Mary-Kate thought. *And I hope she comes back to the group—soon!*

CHAPTER TEN

"Make it stop," Campbell moaned. "Please! Make it stop!"

Mary-Kate turned over in bed and glanced at her clock in the dark. It was 2 A.M.

Every half hour or so, the musical door device had been going off—all by itself. It would play "Jingle Bells" over and over for about five minutes. Mary-Kate couldn't get it to turn off.

"I didn't touch it," Mary-Kate said. "Honest. I didn't even move. It must be triggered by the wind or something."

"I don't care if it's triggered by Santa Claus himself coming into our room!" Campbell said. "I want it to stop!"

Campbell jumped out of bed and picked up the chip from Mary-Kate's desk. She wrapped it in a wool sweater and threw it in the closet.

But when she slammed the closet door, it was still playing.

"Ahhhh!" Campbell cried.

"Sorry," Mary-Kate said for the tenth time that night.

A few minutes later, the music stopped. But Mary-Kate couldn't fall asleep right away. She was still thinking—and worrying—about Penelope.

I hope she liked the bracelet, Mary-Kate thought. *And I hope she liked my note. We really need her in the group.*

Time was running out. Tomorrow was Monday. Only five days left until they had to show the project to the whole school!

I hope Penelope has a good holiday, Mary-Kate thought as she drifted off to sleep. *I hope I don't fail my short-term business class. I hope Carter really likes me. . . .*

When she woke up the next morning, the musical chip was playing "Jingle Bells" again. She and Campbell could hear it through the closet door.

"You're lucky I actually like you," Campbell

said. "Because many roommates have strangled each other over a lot less!"

"I know," Mary-Kate said. "Sorry!"

Mary-Kate didn't even take the musical chip out of the sweater. She left it in the closet and hurried off to breakfast and class.

As soon as she walked into Mr. Meenan's room, she spotted Penelope. She was wearing the sparkly bracelet Mary-Kate had left on her desk.

Yes! Mary-Kate thought. *She likes it!*

"All right, class," Mr. Meenan said. "Let's not waste any time here. Go ahead and get into your groups, so you can work on your projects."

Mary-Kate joined Summer, Justin, Seth, and Carter. They had already staked out the best table in the back of the room.

"Did you talk to her? Is she going to help us?" Summer asked the instant Mary-Kate walked over.

"I didn't exactly talk to her. I left her a note," Mary-Kate explained. "So I don't know."

"She's hanging out over there by herself," Justin said.

"Why didn't you talk to her, anyway?" Carter asked.

"I couldn't find her," Mary-Kate started to say.

But just then Mr. Meenan stopped to chat with

their group. "Well, Mary-Kate, I understand you're the team leader now. Are you ready for Friday?" he asked.

Mary-Kate swallowed hard. "Not yet," she said. "But we will be."

"Well, you have only four days left," Mr. Meenan said sternly. "So get to work!" He turned and walked away.

"Whoa," Summer said. "We're in deep trouble."

"Hey. Here she comes," Carter said, nodding toward Penelope.

Penelope marched over to the group as soon as Meany Meenan was gone. "Listen, Mary-Kate," she said, holding out her arm with the bracelet. "I don't know what you were thinking—but I don't like being bribed with cheap fake jewelry."

"Bribed?" Mary-Kate was shocked. "It wasn't a bribe! I was trying to be nice!"

Penelope laughed a snotty laugh. "Call it whatever you want. But I am not coming back to the group." She spun around, gathered up her books, and marched out of the room.

"I don't believe it!" Mary-Kate said. "I wasn't bribing her. I was—"

"What? Dumping cheap jewelry?" Carter asked.

"No! I was . . ." But she couldn't really explain.

Not the whole story anyway. The stuff about Penelope's mom was private. Penelope would be embarrassed if the whole school knew how her mom was treating her.

"I really didn't think you were that kind of person, Mary-Kate," Carter said coldly.

I'm not! Mary-Kate wanted to say. But her throat was closing up. But she felt as if she might cry.

"Let's just figure out this ad campaign," Summer said, trying to change the subject.

"Yeah," Justin said.

"I wasn't bribing her," Mary-Kate said meekly.

"Whatever," Carter said. "Let's get to work."

For the rest of the period, Mary-Kate struggled to keep calm. She was totally upset. But she led the group and came up with three different ad slogans herself.

Too bad they all stink! she thought.

When the bell rang, Carter shoved back his chair and stood up without even looking at her. He stomped out of the classroom as fast as he could.

Mary-Kate's heart sank.

Now Carter's mad at me. And Penelope's mad at me. And we're all going to fail this project!

She honestly couldn't decide which one of the three was the worst.

CHAPTER ELEVEN

"Ashley! Can I talk to you for a second?" Mary-Kate called across the icy walkway.

Ashley pulled her coat closed tightly. "I've got to go do something really important right now," she called back. "Is it okay if we talk later?"

"I guess. But are you coming to lunch?" Mary-Kate asked. "Because I've had a bad morning."

Lunch? I was going to eat a blueberry muffin left over from breakfast, Ashley thought.

"I don't know," Ashley said. "Are you okay?"

"Sort of," Mary-Kate answered. The wind blew, and she put her hands over her ears. "It's too cold to talk out here."

Ashley shivered. She could tell something was

really bothering her sister. She wanted to stand there on the walkway and find out what was on Mary-Kate's mind. But Mary-Kate was right—it was just too bitterly cold.

"I'll see you at lunch or after school. Okay?" Ashley said.

"Okay," Mary-Kate said, running toward the dining hall.

Ashley ran in the other direction, back toward Porter House. She could hardly wait to complete the errand she was on—returning Cheryl's history notes to her.

She'll be so happy when she sees them! Ashley thought. She had spent three days doing a beautiful job of copying them over. Each section was written with different-colored markers and decorated with stickers. She had even drawn some cartoons in the margins to go with the topics.

This should cheer up Cheryl! Ashley thought. *And then she'll forgive me for ruining her notes in the first place.*

Cheryl had been acting grouchy and angry for days. Just that morning, in the bathroom, she had seemed really upset about something. Ashley heard her tell Campbell that she hadn't gotten any sleep.

"That makes two of us!" Campbell had replied.

Ashley yanked open the front door of Porter House. Samantha was just coming down the stairs of the dorm as Ashley went in.

"Are you coming to the popcorn-stringing contest tonight?" Samantha asked.

"Definitely!" Ashley said happily. She felt so cheery when she thought about all the holiday activities she had planned. The popcorn-stringing contest had been her idea.

Everything about this season is great! Ashley thought. Except for her Secret Santa gifts.

And she was about to make that situation better—right now.

"See you tonight," Samantha called.

"Bye," Ashley called back.

At the top of the stairs, Ashley took off her coat and dropped it in her room. Then she went to Cheryl's room.

She walked softly, so no one would hear her. *I'm just going to sneak in and leave them*, Ashley thought. *That way it will be a nice surprise when Cheryl comes back after class.*

She tiptoed up to Cheryl's door and turned the knob quietly.

"Ahhhhh!" Ashley cried, jumping back.

Cheryl was in there. And the place was a mess!

"What are you doing here?" Ashley blurted out.

Cheryl jumped, startled, and spun around. "I can't find my history notes!" she cried, pulling everything out of her dresser drawers. She stopped. "Wait. What are you doing here? This is my room."

Ashley glanced around the room, stunned. Papers, piles of books, and clothes were lying on the floor and the bed. Cheryl had taken everything out of her desk. Absolutely everything.

Uh-oh. Ashley gulped. "Your history notes?" she said. She held out the beautiful new copies she'd made. "Here they are. I fixed them for you."

"You what?" Cheryl looked horrified.

"I copied them over," Ashley explained. "Because I thought you were mad at me for spilling soda on them. Aren't you happy?"

"Happy? Are you kidding?" Cheryl stared at her. "I've been looking everywhere for those notes! For days!" She sounded furious.

"I'm sor—," Ashley started to say.

"I've been going out of my mind looking for them!" Cheryl went on. "I have to take the history final early because my parents are coming to pick me up on Thursday! I already had less time to study than everyone else. And then when my notes totally disappeared . . . I can't believe you did that, Ashley!"

Ashley gulped again. "I don't know what to say. I mean, I was trying to make it up to you. I knew you were mad at me. I can't believe I made you even madder!"

Cheryl squinted at her. "Mad? What are you talking about? I wasn't mad at you."

"Well, we haven't really hung out all week," Ashley said. "And then you gave me those horrible gifts. I know you're my Secret Santa."

Cheryl shook her head. "No, I'm not," she said.

"You're not?" Ashley's eyes opened wide. She could tell from the look on Cheryl's face that she was telling the truth. She wasn't Ashley's Secret Santa. "Oh."

Cheryl shook her head again and tried to calm down. "Look, I guess you were trying to be nice. And the new notes are really pretty. But I've really got to study now. Okay?"

"Sure," Ashley said, backing out of the room. "I'm sorry," she added again.

Out in the hall, Ashley just stood there for a minute. What a bummer! She had been trying to do a nice thing—and it backfired.

I'll have to make it up to her somehow, Ashley thought. *I'll get her a really nice Secret Santa gift for her last day.*

But still, Ashley felt terrible.

If Cheryl wasn't her Secret Santa . . .

If Cheryl didn't give her those stinky, terrible gifts . . .

Then who did?

CHAPTER TWELVE

Mary-Kate grabbed a tray in the dining hall and went through the line. Boiled beef. Stewed tomatoes. Salami sandwiches. Grapefruit slices. Rice pudding.

How is it possible? she wondered. *How could they serve all the foods I hate—on the same day?*

She took a salami sandwich, a bowl of grapefruit slices, and some rice pudding. Then she sat down by herself.

What a terrible holiday season! she thought.

She had missed out on almost all the fun. There had been only one good thing this month—Carter Black. And now he was mad at her.

And for what? For trying to make Penelope's holiday a little better.

She took a bite of a grapefruit slice. It was extra sour.

Can anything else bad happen? she wondered.

"Hi," someone said, coming up behind her.

Mary-Kate looked up. It was Summer, carrying her lunch tray. She had a peanut butter sandwich and a carton of chocolate milk.

"Where did you get that?" Mary-Kate asked, staring at the food.

"The cafeteria lady likes me," Summer said, grinning. "I told her I'm a vegetarian, so she made me a PB and J. And she went in the back and gave me the last carton of chocolate milk."

"But you're not a vegetarian, are you?" Mary-Kate asked.

Summer shook her long blond hair. "No. But she doesn't know that. She's got a bad memory."

Mary-Kate almost laughed, but not quite. She was too down in the dumps.

"Guess what?" Summer announced, sounding excited. "I know who your Secret Santa is!"

"That's nice." Mary-Kate picked at her pudding.

"Don't you want to know who it is?" Summer sounded surprised.

Mary-Kate shrugged. "No," she said. "Don't tell me."

"I can't believe you!" Summer said. "You've been getting the best presents in the whole dorm!"

That's true, Mary-Kate thought. First the baseball cards. Then a huge tin of caramel corn. Then the bracelet.

"But I didn't get anything today," Mary-Kate pointed out. "Besides—it's supposed to be a surprise."

"Yes, but in this case, I think you'll want to know," Summer said. Her eyes danced.

"No, I won't," Mary-Kate asked. "Why would I?"

"Because it's Carter Black!" Summer blurted out. She beamed at Mary-Kate.

"Carter?" Mary-Kate's mouth dropped open. She let her spoon fall with a plop into her rice pudding.

Summer nodded. "He told Justin and Justin told Samantha and Samantha told me."

No wonder he was so mad at me! Mary-Kate thought. *I gave his bracelet away!*

In a rush, she pushed away from the table and scrambled into her coat. "I've got to go," she said.

"What's wrong?" Summer said. "Aren't you glad?"

"I'll explain later!" Mary-Kate called as she dashed out of the dining hall.

Her mind raced, trying to think about Carter's schedule.

Didn't I see Carter going to a drumming class at the Student U yesterday? Mary-Kate thought. *Right before lunch?*

Mary-Kate ran across campus in the cold. The Student U wasn't far, but the wind was brutal today. By the time she reached the building, her face was bright red and stinging.

She yanked open the door.

Empty! Everyone was gone—except for Mr. Murphy, who taught the class.

"May I help you?" Mr. Murphy said.

"Um, I was looking for someone in your drumming class," Mary-Kate replied. "Sorry to interrupt."

"That's all right," Mr. Murphy said. "I let them out early."

"Thanks." Mary-Kate ran back outside. Her heart was pounding. She had to find Carter!

Where did he go? she wondered. Then she saw a group of guys in the distance. They were waiting at the Harrington shuttle bus stop. And Carter was with them!

Mary-Kate sprinted over there.

"Carter, can I talk to you?" Mary-Kate said, racing up to him.

He glanced away from the group. "What?"

"I know you're my Secret Santa," she said. "And

I know why you're mad at me—for giving the bracelet to Penelope. But there's a good reason."

"What reason?" Carter asked. He still looked angry, but his face was a little bit softer. He stepped away from the other boys.

"I love my presents!" Mary-Kate said, talking quickly. "Everything you gave me was perfect. And the bracelet was the best!"

She looked into his eyes and tried to let him see she really meant what she was saying.

"Then why did you give it away?" Carter asked.

Should I tell him? Mary-Kate wondered. She knew she shouldn't reveal stuff about Penelope's private life.

But he sounds so hurt! Mary-Kate thought. *I've got to tell him the truth.*

"It's a long story," she said quickly. "I went to Penelope's room to talk to her, remember? About coming back to the group."

Carter nodded.

"And I saw this e-mail lying on her desk," Mary-Kate went on. "It was from her mom—and it was awful! Her mom isn't coming home for the holidays. She's shipping Penelope off to some island with her great-aunt."

"Wow. That's terrible," Carter said.

Mary-Kate nodded. "Anyway, when I read that, I thought a beautiful present might cheer her up. That's why I gave her the bracelet. I just wanted her to be happy."

Carter gave her a sweet smile. "That was nice," he said. "I thought you didn't like it. I didn't really think you would bribe her or anything."

"No way," Mary-Kate said. "I'd never do that. I loved it."

The bus pulled up to the stop.

"I've got to go," Carter said. But he sounded as if he didn't want to.

Mary-Kate leaned forward and gave him a quick hug. "I loved my presents," she said again.

"Good," he said as he climbed on the bus. "I'll e-mail you. Okay?"

Yes! Mary-Kate thought, smiling. *He likes me! I can tell.*

She shivered. It was still freezing outside, even though she felt all warm and happy inside. She turned to hurry back to the dining hall—and gasped.

Penelope was standing right behind her. She had heard every word Mary-Kate had said.

And she didn't look happy!

75

CHAPTER THIRTEEN

"How dare you read my private mail!" Penelope said.

"I know I shouldn't have," Mary-Kate said. "I just . . ."

The wind blew, making Mary-Kate shiver again. She was so cold, her teeth were chattering. She gestured back toward the warm dining hall.

"Can we go in?" Mary-Kate said.

Penelope nodded and they both hurried inside.

"I'm sorry," Mary-Kate as she pulled open the door to the dining hall. "I didn't mean to snoop. I just saw the letter by accident, when I was—"

"Never mind," Penelope said. "I understand. You were trying to be nice."

"Yes," Mary-Kate nodded. "Honestly, I was. I just wanted to give you a present so you wouldn't be left out of the holidays."

Penelope smiled. Then she did something that totally surprised Mary-Kate. She hugged her!

"Thank you," Penelope said. "That's the nicest thing anyone has done for me since I came here to White Oak."

"Really?" Mary-Kate said.

"Yes." Then Penelope slipped the bracelet off her arm. "But you should take it back."

"Oh, no, I . . ." Mary-Kate didn't know what to do. She wanted the bracelet—especially now that she knew Carter had given it to her! But she didn't want to take back something after she'd given it away.

"No, take it," Penelope insisted. "Carter gave it to you—not me." She smiled. "And you like him, don't you?"

Mary-Kate blushed and took the bracelet. She slipped it on. "Yeah."

"He's cute," Penelope agreed. "So how's the project coming?"

"Not great," Mary-Kate admitted. "We've gotten a lot of the charts done, and all the math stuff. But we really need help with the ad campaign. Would you be willing to come back?"

Penelope thought about it for a minute. Then she shrugged and laughed. "Why not?" she said. "It would be more fun than what I've been doing!"

"Seriously? What have you been doing?" Mary-Kate asked.

"Going to the library and rereading *A Christmas Carol*," Penelope said.

"You mean that book about Scrooge?" Mary-Kate asked.

Penelope nodded and giggled. "I was looking for some grumpy lines to use on you. But somehow 'Bah, humbug' didn't sound too realistic!"

Mary-Kate laughed really hard. She didn't know Penelope had a sense of humor! "It would be great if you'd come back to the group. We could be co-leaders. I'll bet we'd come up with an awesome project together!"

"So when is your next meeting?" Penelope asked.

"Summer and I were going to work on the project today in the dorm, after last period," Mary-Kate said.

"Let's meet in my room," Penelope offered. "And I'll bring the popcorn—just so we won't miss out on all the holiday fun!"

The Perfect Gift

The meeting in Penelope's room was super. The boys couldn't come, of course. They weren't allowed in the girls' dorm. But Mary-Kate, Summer, and Penelope came up with three great ad slogans. Then they got on-line to chat with Justin, Seth, and Carter about it.

"Carter likes Penelope's slogan," Summer reported. "So does Justin."

She was at Penelope's desk, doing the typing.

"Okay, it's settled, then," Mary-Kate said. "We're using Penelope's idea, 'Open the door to the sounds of Christmas.'"

"It's simple but convincing," Summer said. "I love it."

"Yay!" Mary-Kate cheered. It was such a relief to have the ad campaign settled!

"Seth says he loves it, too" Summer reported. "He's going to put the slogan on all the marketing reports." She clicked the mouse. "They have to get to work now."

"Oh, don't sign off yet!" Penelope said. She leaned over Summer's shoulder. "I want to say something to the boys before they leave."

"Go ahead." Summer stood up. "I've got to get busy on the posters anyway. But all our poster board is in my room."

"I'll come help in a minute," Mary-Kate called. When Summer was gone, she asked Penelope, "What are you typing to the boys?"

"Oh, just an apology," Penelope explained. "To let them know I'm sorry I've been such a grouch."

"That's nice. It's always a good idea to let people know how you feel," Mary-Kate said. "And I had an idea about that—something I wanted to talk to you about."

"What?" Penelope asked.

"I was thinking," Mary-Kate said. "Why don't you send your mom an e-mail? Let her know how you feel about being alone for the holidays."

Penelope sagged in the chair. "She's so busy," she said. "She won't care."

"She's not too busy to read an e-mail," Mary-Kate said. "At least it's worth a try."

"Do you think?" Penelope had a hopeful look on her face.

"Definitely!" Mary-Kate said.

"Mary-Kate!"

Huh? Mary-Kate rolled over in bed the next morning and pulled the covers up to her chin.

Someone was knocking on her door. But it was still dark outside!

What time is it, anyway? she wondered. She glanced at her clock. Six A.M.?

"Go away," Campbell moaned from her bed.

"Mary-Kate!" the voice called softly outside her door again.

Who is that? Mary-Kate wondered sleepily. Then she woke up enough to realize. It was someone with a British accent.

Penelope!

Mary-Kate climbed out of bed and slipped on her robe. Quietly, she tiptoed into the hall.

Penelope was standing there in her nightgown.

"What's wrong?" she asked.

"I'm sorry to wake you," Penelope said. "But I couldn't wait to tell you. My mom just called!"

"At this hour?" Mary-Kate yawned.

"It's six o'clock at night in Hong Kong," Penelope explained. "And she forgot. Anyway, guess what? She's coming home for Christmas! And it's all thanks to you!"

"Really?" Suddenly Mary-Kate was wide awake. "That's awesome!" She gave Penelope a hug.

Penelope was so excited, she was bouncing. "I sent her an e-mail, just like you said. And she called me the minute she received it! She was very sorry. She said she didn't know how lonely I was."

"I'm so glad," Mary-Kate said.

"I just got off the phone," Penelope babbled on, "and I couldn't go back to sleep. I had to tell you."

Wow, Mary-Kate thought. *That's the best present I've gotten so far this year. And it wasn't even for me!*

"Miss Viola was already awake when the phone rang—thank goodness," Penelope went on.

Miss Viola was the dorm mother. Her room was on the first floor. She answered the phone in the hall when the girls were asleep.

"Anyway, she's making me a cup of tea to drink in the lounge," Penelope said. "Would you like one?"

Tea? Mary-Kate wasn't used to drinking tea. But Penelope was English. She drank tea all the time.

"Sure," Mary-Kate said, following Penelope downstairs. "Why not?"

"Guess what else?" Penelope said as they walked down the steps. "My mom is going to be here by Friday morning—in time for the big assembly, when we present our projects!"

"Cool," Mary-Kate said.

Penelope stopped at the bottom of the stairs. "It's more than cool," she said. "This is the best Christmas I've had in years! And it wouldn't have happened without you, Mary-Kate. I know it's really corny to say this, but you've brought Christmas back to me. And I thank you with all my heart."

Mary-Kate couldn't stop grinning. *Wow*, she thought. *Talk about feeling the holiday spirit! Does it get any better than this?*

CHAPTER FOURTEEN

"Can you believe he gave us all A's?" Mary-Kate asked, bouncing up and down.

"I know!" Summer said. "I thought I was dreaming. Meany Meenan actually seemed proud of us."

The big assembly on Friday had just ended. Mary-Kate and her group had shown their Jingle Bells Door Opener. The other groups had displayed their holiday sales projects, too.

Now both girls scanned the auditorium, looking for Penelope.

"Good job, Mary-Kate," Mr. Meenan said, patting her on the shoulder as he walked through the crowd. "You made an excellent leader."

"Thanks." Mary-Kate grinned.

"He's just trying to butter you up," Summer whispered, "so you'll sign up for his short-term class in the spring. Don't fall for it."

Mary-Kate laughed. Summer was probably right.

"Hey, there she is," Mary-Kate said, pointing to Penelope.

"We should thank her again," Summer said. "I mean, 'Open the Door to Christmas' was such a hit. Everyone cheered when we showed the ad campaign."

"I know," Mary-Kate said. "But she's with her mom now. I don't want to interrupt."

"Okay," Summer agreed. "I want to get over to the Student U anyway. Today is when we find out who our Secret Santas are!"

Right, Mary-Kate thought. *Except I already know who mine is!*

Mary-Kate was still excited. She had one more gift for Ross. It was a baby picture of Ashley—with peanut butter all over her face and hair!

He should like that, Mary-Kate thought. For one thing, it was cute. And for another, he could always use it to blackmail Ashley—whenever she got too bossy!

Mary-Kate couldn't wait to give it to him.

Ashley stood on a chair at the back of the Student U. "Okay, everyone, this is the big moment," she announced. "Time for all you Secret Santas to come forward—and give your last gifts—and reveal your true identities!"

All the White Oak girls and Harrington boys were there. Almost every person had a gift of some sort in his or her hands.

"Then afterward, we're having a doughnut and hot cider party," she said. "So don't go anywhere." The crowd cheered.

"Okay, ready?" Ashley asked. "On the count of three. One . . . two . . . three!"

All at once, the place was a madhouse. People were pushing and shoving to reach the person they had a present for.

I'll just stand here, Ashley thought. *And wait. That way my Secret Santa can find me easily!*

Besides, she didn't have a gift for Cheryl today. Cheryl had gone home early. As her last gift, Ashley had given her a red-and-white-striped sock filled with candy canes.

Cheryl was a candy-cane freak. She had loved it. Ashley stood watching. Waiting.

How come no one's coming toward me? she wondered.

From her perch, she could see Dana giving Megan a caramel apple. She also saw Ross giving a whoopee cushion to Marty Silver. Then she saw Mary-Kate giving Ross something in a frame.

"Hey!" Ashley cried, jumping down. "Is that a picture of me?" She ran over to Ross.

"You were such a cute baby!" Ross said, smiling at the picture. "Messy eater, but cute."

"Give me that!" Ashley said.

"Don't do it, Ross!" Mary-Kate teased. "That picture will come in handy someday. Take my word for it!"

Someone tapped Ashley on the shoulder. She turned around. It was her cousin Jeremy.

"What's up?" Ashley asked.

Jeremy pulled a small wrapped box out from behind his back. "Happy holidays," he said, handing it to her.

"Who's this from?" Ashley demanded. "My Secret Santa is supposed to . . ."

Then she saw the sneaky grin on Jeremy's face. All at once it hit her.

"Oh, no!" she said. "Not you!"

"Ha, ha, ha, ha, ha!" Jeremy laughed. He clearly thought he was a genius. "I got you, didn't I?"

"I should have known," Ashley said. "No one

but you would give me a stinky old sock! Or a half-eaten sandwich! Or a piece of coal!"

"That was the best part!" Jeremy bragged, still laughing. "When I pretended I was delivering that coal for someone else! Brilliant, huh?"

Ooh! Ashley thought. For a minute, she was so mad she wanted to drown him in the punch bowl!

"You are so not funny, Jeremy," she said, putting her hands on her hips.

Jeremy looked a little hurt. He pointed to the small box in her hands. "Open it," he said.

"Why," Ashley said. "Is there a tarantula in it or something?"

"Just open it," Jeremy insisted.

Okay, Ashley thought. *Why not? How bad could it be?*

She tore off the wrapping paper quickly and lifted the lid.

"Oh, wow!" She stared at her gift—a cool pair of dangling earrings, with shiny black and silver beads. They were perfect.

"You like?" Jeremy asked.

Ashley nodded. "They're great." She gave him a big smile. "Okay, I forgive you."

"Happy holidays," Jeremy said again, and this time he sounded like he meant it.

"Happy holidays to you," Ashley told her cousin.

She felt all warm and fuzzy inside. The Secret Santa had been a big success. And now the term was over—and everyone was going home.

Yes, Ashley thought. *Happy holidays to all—and to all a good break!*

COOL RUNNINGS

by Elise Van Hook

Over the river (okay, the creek) and through the woods, to Harrington we went on Saturday night! A great time was had by all at the White Oak/ Harrington Swingin' Sleigh Ride.

Due to a huge turnout, Harrington's antique sleighs couldn't keep up with all the people who wanted to ride them. What's a student to do?

Thanks to the quick thinking of Phoebe Cahill, emergency "sleighs" were called in to save the evening. Were they really sleighs? Nah. But no one even recognized the White Oak Maintenance Service trucks decorated for the occasion by Madame LeBlanc's Sew What? fashion elective class. I guess *some* electives came in handy this semester!

GLAM GAB
Party in Style!
by Ashley Burke

Fashion expert Ashley Burke

So what are *your* big plans for December 31? Watching the ball drop on TV all by yourself? Well, throw those purple jammies and oh-so-flattering White Oak sweats way back in your closet. You're not wearing them this New Year's Eve!

In fact, here's a New Year's Resolution for you: NO MORE BORING NEW YEARS! Send all your buds back home an e-mail right this second and invite them for a rockin' eve at your house. Stuck for original party ideas? Here are two you might want to try.

—**The Great Resolution Kickoff Party:** Don't want to stick to your own resolutions? How about sticking to someone else's? Have each guest write down her favorite (and hardest) resolution on a slip of paper. Put all the slips into a bowl. Take turns picking someone else's resolution—and try to keep it for the next year. (And no trading!)
—**The Endless Summer Party:** Caught the January blues? Warm yourself up

with a summer shindig! Ask guests to dress in beach attire. (Sarongs and instant tanner are good accessories!) Pass out Hawaiian leis and pineapple juice at the door. Put down blankets or towels and turn up the heat full blast. Play the CDs you burned with last summer's top tunes—and *party*! (Do not attempt to create your own beach

with sand from your little sister's sandbox. Your parents might not be too thrilled.)

Start off the year by partying in style!

THE GET-REAL GIRL

Dear Get-Real Girl,

I am so totally furious! I went out on a date with this guy I met in the Student U. But the guy I met wasn't the guy I went out with. It was his twin brother! They thought it was a big joke. I never should have talked to

them in the first place—they are such huge losers! How can I get back at them?

Signed,
Double-Steamed

Dear Double-Steamed,

Try not to take it too hard. If it was a first date, how

were you supposed to know the guy had a twin? But look at it this way, DS. You already got back at them. Now everyone knows what jerks they are!

Signed,
Get-Real Girl

Dear Get-Real Girl,

My problem is soooo embarrassing. My roommate says I talk in my sleep and always wake her up. I didn't believe her, but she made a tape recording to prove it. The crazy thing is, I say things that aren't even true! Last night I talked about how I love this geeky guy in my class so much that I'll do anything for him—including

feeding him his food. And now it's on her tape for everyone to hear. Help!

Signed,
Big Mouth

Dear Big Mouth,

Can I have a copy of that tape? Just kidding. I'm sure your roommate understands that you can't help it. Maybe you should get her a pair of earplugs, or she could wear head-phones to bed. As for talk-ing in your sleep—you're on your own with that one. (Just make sure you get rid of the incriminating evidence!)

Signed,
Get-Real Girl

HOLIDAY HOOP-LA
by Mary-Kate Burke

What better way to spend a chilly Saturday after-

Sports pro Mary-Kate Burke

noon than playing your favorite sport? B-ball, v-ball, t-ball—last week we had our pick when Harrington hosted their Annual Winter Sports Marathon!

But we're not talking the usual sporting events here. Students from White Oak and Harrington were kicking, running, and jumping—holiday style!

The Jingle Bell Relay was a huge crowd-pleaser. Instead of a baton, the runners passed jingle bells! A few time-outs were called during the Cocoa Bear-Walk

to mop up spills. I guess most of the contestants

couldn't carry a cup full of cocoa in their mouths and walk on their hands at the same time! The White Oak Winter Coats zipped up the Harrington Hats in the day's final event, the Candy-Cane Shoot-out. Instead of throwing basketballs through the hoop,

the players threw candy canes!

Unfortunately, this reporter has been forced to bring you the action secondhand.

She had to miss the coolest sporting event of the year because she was in the library working on a project for a certain fall elective. But it sounded like so much fun that she will definitely be there next year!

THE FIRST-FORM BUZZ
by Dana Woletsky

What better way to deal with freezing cold than HOT HOT gossip?

It seems that practically every single person in Mr. M's elective class made Santa's "bad" list this year. Rumor is they forgot to put in enough time at the North Pole (a.k.a. library)!

PM managed to make the "good" list. But as far as whether she was naughty or nice, you'd have to ask MKB . . . .

By the way, CB, have you noticed the way MKB has been looking at you lately? Because everyone else in her study group has!

Speaking of Santas, unless you're living under a snowball, you know that the campus has been invaded by Secret Santas. But someone with the initials AB has a Secret Santa that doesn't like  her . . . and I don't blame her Santa one bit!

Remember—if you want the juicy holiday scoop, all you gotta do is snoop!

UPCOMING CALENDAR
Fall/Winter

February is an important month for the Harrington

School: It's their big 1-5-0 birthday! That many years of guys next door to White Oak is really something to celebrate. So make a note on your calendar *now* for the Founders Day Ball on Saturday the 23rd.

Come on, admit it! You know you're going to miss your roomie over winter break. Leave her a good-bye note on the See-You-Next-Semester Message Board at the Student Union and let her know you care. (Sniff!)

Hearts? Flowers? Sappy cards and chocolate kiss-es? V-Day is coming up faster than you can pack away your candy canes! It's never too early to start planning a surprise for your special someone. Stay tuned to *The Acorn* for details on Valentine's Day events, or see Ashley Burke for late-breaking love-connection details.

If getting in shape tops your New Year's resolution list, the P.E. Department can help! Dance Til You Drop classes will be held at the main gym every

Wednesday during January at 7:30 p.m. Wear your favorite socks and be ready to jitterbug, swing, and get jazzed.

IT'S ALL IN THE STARS
Fall Horoscopes

Scorpio
(Oct. 24-Nov. 21)

You're always thinking of doing nice things for other people—and this time of year is especially stressful. After all, Scorpios insist on getting their friends and family the perfect gifts! But don't despair. Go to the mall. The answers will come to you!

Sagittarius
(Nov. 22-Dec. 21)

Suddenly you're the center of attention. Enjoy it! But be warned: People are listening to every word you say. Try hard not to let any important holiday secrets slip. Your best bud is counting on you. And you may soon have an exciting secret of your own to share with her!

Capricorn
(Dec. 22-Jan. 19)

Holiday spirits suddenly fizzled? You probably need a break. Make popcorn, watch a video, take a nap. Or dance around your room with your toothbrush and a towel on your head. You'll need plenty of energy for fun times ahead!

PSST! Take a sneak peek
at

#27: The Facts
About Flirting

"This is crazy," Ashley exclaimed, standing under an oak tree on campus. "We actually found the Tree of Love!"

"I know," Phoebe replied. "Can you believe that love letters were exchanged in this very tree over one hundred fifty years ago?"

Ashley pointed to the tree trunk. "That hole is perfect for holding love letters. We should give this baby a test run!"

"We need to find someone who is madly in love with a guy but too shy to tell him," Phoebe said.

The two girls thought for a second.

Then Ashley hit her forehead with the palm of her hand. "Duh!" she exclaimed. "Mary-Kate likes her fencing partner, Jordan, but is too shy to flirt with him. The tree is the perfect way to bring them together!"

"What should we do?" Phoebe asked.

"Well," Ashley said, "I can write an unsigned love letter to Jordan and ask him to leave his answer in the tree."

Phoebe's dark curls bounced as she nodded. "And when Jordan responds—you can slip that letter to Mary-Kate!"

Ashley's heart beat faster as she thought her plan through. "Then Mary-Kate will write the next letter and so on and so on," she declared. "Until Mary-Kate and Jordan are so in love that they have to meet—and the rest is history!"

"Brilliant!" Phoebe cried. "We'll be bringing Mary-Kate together with the boy of her dreams and she won't even know it!"

"Now remember," Ashley said, "not a word about the love letters to Mary-Kate. We don't want to make her nervous."

"This is too wild!" Phoebe exclaimed. "Do you think it's going to work?"

"Hey, it worked a century ago," Ashley replied. "Come on, Phoebe. We've got a letter to write!"

The Ultimate Fa...

mary-kat...

Don't miss

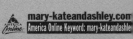

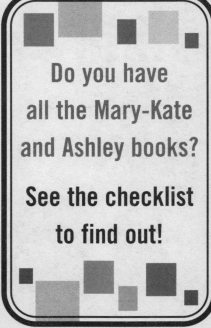